Brenda Tibingana

Samuel and the Bapa

A little boy with a choice to make

 FriesenPress

Suite 300 - 990 Fort St
Victoria, BC, V8V 3K2
Canada

www.friesenpress.com

ISBN
978-1-5255-9001-6 (Hardcover)
978-1-5255-9000-9 (Paperback)
978-1-5255-9002-3 (eBook)

1. *Juvenile Fiction, Fantasy & Magic*

Distributed to the trade by The Ingram Book Company

For Mwine and Khwezi, I love you. And Asa...
Thank you! BTA

Samuel was four years old and he enjoyed many things.

He loved to read with

his Mummy and Daddy.

He loved to play catch with his sister Tina

and he loved to play in the park.

Best of all, he loved to visit
the imaginary zoo in his back yard.
His favorite zoo animal was a Bapa
Have you ever seen a Bapa at the zoo?
Well, you can see one at the zoo at Samuel's house.
A Bapa is as big as a goat and has a duck-shaped body.
It stands on four legs, has a face of a cat and a peacock tail.
The Bapa at the zoo at Samuel's house was always quiet.
It never made a sound. Samuel spoke for it.
"The Bapa is hungry today. He has not eaten.
I think he would like a cookie and some ice-cream."

Samuel loved many things but he also disliked many things. When
asked to do something he did not like, he always said, "I don't want to."
For example, when his Mummy asked,
"Are you going to finish up that broccoli?" Samuel said,
I don't want to," shaking his head.

In the bathroom, his Daddy said, "Say Ahh," as he tried to get Samuel to open his mouth and brush his teeth. Samuel clenched his teeth and said, "I don't want to!"

When he found Tina reading his book one day, he reached out and grabbed it from her, "That's my book!" Samuel said.

"Share!" Tina said, but Samuel turned and ran away with the book "I don't want to!" he said. And on it went, every day:

"I don't want to." "I don't want to!" "I don't want to!!"

One afternoon, Samuel and Tina were playing in the park.

"It's time to go home!" Mummy said.

"I don't want to go home," Samuel whined.

He ran off to the slides again.

At the slide, he saw a strange animal standing on the first step.
He stared at it. It was as big as a goat, and had a duck-shaped body.
It stood on four legs, and had the face of a cat and a peacock tail.

"Huh?" gasped Samuel, wide eyed. "A Bapa?"
The animal bobbed its head up and down.
"Bapas are not real," he whispered. "They are pretend animals.
Only for pretend play." "I am real," the Bapa said.
"You speak?" Samuel gasped and looked around to see if the voice
came from someone else. But no one seemed to notice.
"Bapas don't speak." He said looking at the Bapa again.
"I speak only when I have to," the Bapa replied. "Your mummy said it
is time to go home. You should listen to her."
"I don't want to." Samuel said.
"Did you know," said the Bapa, "that everything we do,
has consequences?"
"Con......? What does that mean?" said Samuel
"It means that if we respect others and are kind, then we grow.
If we don't, then we shrink." said the Bapa
"I don't want to talk to you," Samuel said.
"You don't want to grow? Maybe you would like to shrink instead."
The Bapa said smiling.

"Samuel," he heard his mother calling again.

"It's time to go!"

"Last one home cleans up after dinner."
Tina yelled to him and dashed off.
"Not fair," Samuel yelled back as he run after her.

"That is on your chore chart."

That night, Samuel was the first at the table.

He pushed aside the broccoli on his plate.

He did not want it to touch his rice and chicken.

"I don't want to eat those,"

he said quietly.

As soon as he said it, he felt a tingling all over his body. Soon, he became shorter and shorter and smaller and smaller. He was still four years old, but he could not see the top of the table anymore.

"Samuel?" Mummy called when she came to the table

"Samuel!" she called again.

"Where is that boy?"

"Samuel, I need you at the table."

"I'm right here, Mummy," he said in his little voice.

"No games tonight Samuel. Where are you?" she asked again when she walked away looking for him. Soon everyone was searching the whole house for him. "Right here" he said louder.

He was afraid and sad and no one could hear him no matter how loud he spoke. Then he remembered the Bapa's words in the park:

"Maybe you would like to shrink."

"Oh no . . . I don't . . ." he said quietly. "I'll take just one bite of that broccoli." He climbed the back of his chair then sat on the table next to his plate and reached for the broccoli.

As he ate, he realized broccoli was not so bad.
Then he felt very warm all over his body and a gentle tugging on his arms and
legs that tickled his feet. This made him laugh loud. Soon everyone came back
and found him seated on the table.

"Why are you laughing?" Tina asked

"Where have you been?" His mummy asked. "We were looking all over for you. Please sit in your chair" She added.

"I was under the table. I had shrunk." He said when he had settled in his chair "These games must stop Samuel!" his daddy said.

"Now our dinner is cold."

"I wasn't playing games Daddy." Samuel said sadly.

"Let's eat." His mummy said as they all sat at the table.

His mummy looked at his plate then looked at him "Samuel, where did you hide your broccoli?" She said

"I ate it." He replied

"Did you really eat the broccoli?" she asked.

"It's not so bad" he said.

"Wow, Samuel! Good for you!" his mummy said.

The next day, Samuel opened the door to go outside to play.

"You will need to put on some shoes." Mummy said.

"I don't want to," he said, and he went off outside. "Ouch!" he shouted

as he stepped on a prickly spruce branch. "Ouch!!!"

He felt tingling all over his body like before. He watched as a butterfly,

ants and the grass all became bigger than him.

"Why is everything bigger than me?"

"Maybe you would like to shrink." He remembered. "No!"

"Mummy, where are my shoes?" he called as he walked back to the

house. He felt a tickle and started to laugh and everything became its

normal size again

That night, he clenched his teeth together.

He wouldn't let Daddy brush them.

Just as he was about to say, "I don't want to brush my teeth,"

he remembered the Bapa. He turned to face his daddy.

"I can brush my teeth, Daddy." he said.

"You brush first, and I finish up" Daddy said.

"Okay," Samuel said, and he started to brush his teeth.

When he was done, he gave Daddy his toothbrush

and opened his mouth. "Ahhh . . ." he said.

"You are growing," Daddy said.

Strange—Samuel did feel a little taller

He felt taller when he shared his book and toys with Tina.

He felt taller when he let the other kids have

a go on swings at the park.

When Mummy said, "It's time to go home,"

he turned to Tina and shouted,

"Last one home sets the table" then he raced home.